ANYA BELTSINA

SMILEY, HAPPY PLANET EARTH

OUR PLANET

One day children came to class.
Their teacher kindly asked:
"Where do we live, my friends?"
He saw rows of small, raised hands.

All the kids said, "In the cities,
in the houses, so pretty."
Their teacher told them all
that their subject was the world.

"You all live on planet Earth!
A special place in the Universe.
It comes third after the sun.
It's the home for everyone:
human beings, reptiles, trees,
birds, small insects just like bees.

4

"Earth consists of lots of places
that have life in all their spaces.
Other planets look so nice,
but some of them are cold as ice.

5

"Both Neptune and Uranus
are the coldest of the planets.

"Earth has seven continents.
They have animals and plants.

"Earth is known far and wide
as a 'blue planet' with huge tides.
Earth is covered by the oceans.
Gravity sets tides in motion."

All the children in the class
raised their hands, and then they asked:

"How large is our planet?"
"Is it more dense than hard granite?"

"Is Earth round as a ball?"
"Can we live in the North Pole?"

Their teacher listened well.
There was a lot to tell.
He explained that planet Earth,
a special place in the Universe,
is much larger than red Mars,
but much smaller than most stars.

CRUST

MANTLE

OUTER
CORE

INNER
CORE

"Earth is made of four thick coats.
Children, are you taking notes?!
Outer core and inner core.
Wait a minute! There is more!
Crust and mantle — words to know.
Crust on top, the rest below.

"If we look at Earth from space,
we can see most colorful place.
Blue, white, brown, yellow, and green
are the colors to be seen."

That day children learned in class:
Earth is a sphere and has a great mass.
All kids learned that planet Earth
is the best in the Universe!

PLANET EARTH

SEASONS

Next day's subject was four seasons.
These great seasons have their reasons.

When the North Pole tilts toward the sun,
it is hot for everyone
in the Northern Hemisphere.
Summer time comes with a cheer!
Everyone in Northern part
can sunbathe in one's backyard.
When the South Pole is inclined,
winter comes with less sunshine.
Happy kids ski, skate, and slide
on the sparkling ice they glide.

WINTER

AUTUMN

17

Four great seasons never meet.
They cannot just chat and greet.
Fall time never meets with spring.
Summer never feels frost sting.

Just imagine if they meet
that fun chat can sound sweet.
Winter, being bitter cold,
is the most brave and bold.
Winter season may tell all:
"I make heavy snow fall.
I force gust and wind to blow,
cover fields and lakes with snow."

Spring can sing another song:
"I make daytime grow so long!
I bring flowers and plants.
I help birds to sing fine chants!"

Summer season may just laugh:
"I am filled with fun cool stuff!
My bright sunshine is the best!
I bring pleasure, joy and zest!"

Fall can boast and brag to all:
"I force leaves to shed and fall.
My trees' colors are so bright!
I bring harvest with delight!"

It is fun to greet the seasons!
Every season has its reasons.
They all bring us different foods.
Fall presents us with ripe fruit.

Winter parties
and celebrations
bring sweet treats
and recreation.

Spring is time
for plants and herbs,
flowers
at every curb.

Beltsina Anya.
Smiley, Happy Planet Earth. – 2021. – 28 p.

....

Book for children

6+

By Anya Beltsina
SMILEY, HAPPY PLANET EARTH

Illustrations by Kristina Yolkina

Ordering Information:
For details, contact theanyabeltsina@gmail.com.

Print ISBN: 978-1-66780-714-0

Printed in the United States of America.

First Edition